The Child's World of
SUCCESS

Library of Congress Cataloging-in-Publication Data

McDonnell, Janet, 1962-
Success / Janet McDonnell.
p.   cm.
Summary: Simple text and scenes depict such successful experiences as
finishing a puzzle with fifty pieces, winning an award for the
Halloween costume that you and Mom made, learning to whistle, and
finding a way to have fun on a rainy day.
Originally published: c1988.
ISBN 1-56766-294-3 (hardcover)
1. Success in children—Juvenile literature.   [1. Success.]
I. Title.
[BF723.S77M33   1996]
158'.1—dc20   96-11837
                               CIP
                               AC

The Child's World of
SUCCESS

By Janet McDonnell • Illustrated by Mechelle Ann

THE CHILD'S WORLD

When you try very hard and are finally able to say, "I did it!"—that's success.

Success is painting a picture that makes you happy and proud.

Winning an award for the Halloween costume that you and Mom made—that's success!

Success is teaching your little sister the alphabet.

Success is practicing a song for the winter program over and over and then singing it the best you can on the night of the program.

When you save your allowance week after week, and finally have enough money to buy a new truck—that's success!

Success is finding your friend during a game of hide-and-go-seek. And it's hiding so well that your friend can't find you!

Success is finding a way to have fun on a rainy day.

And success is finding out that the boat you and Dad built really does float!

When your brother teaches you to make brownies, and everyone says, "Delicious!"—that's success.

Success is when you open a book and say, "I can read it myself, Mom."

Success is reaching a goal. It's finishing a task.
It's doing the best you can do.

Can you think of other ways to be successful?